For Louis and Freya
and anyone else who is a bit worried.
J.S.

For every child waiting for a new brother or sister
F.C.

First published in Great Britain in 2009 by Gullane Children's Books
This paperback edition published 2010 by

Gullane Children's Books
185 Fleet Street, London, EC4A 2HS
www.gullanebooks.com

2   4   6   8   10   9   7   5   3   1

Text © Jonathan Shipton 2009
Illustrations © Francesca Chessa 2009

The right of Jonathan Shipton and Francesca Chessa to be identified as the author and illustrator of this
work has been asserted by them in accordance with the Copyright, Designs and Patents Act, 1988.

A CIP record for this title is available from the British Library.

ISBN: 978-1-86233-779-4

Printed and bound in China

This book belongs to:

_____

_____

Baby Baby blah blah blah!

Jonathan Shipton

illustrated by

Francesca Chessa

GULLANE
CHILDREN'S BOOKS

Emily loved to make lists.
She made lists of things she didn't like.
She made lists of things she loved.
And sometimes she made lists of worries.

One day Emily's mum and dad said,
"Guess what? We're going to have a . . .

...baby!"

"Oh," said Emily. "That's nice."
And she carried on playing
with her guinea pig.

That night Emily said,
"You know this baby, is it going
to be a brother or a sister?"
"It's going to be a surprise," said Emily's dad.
"I'd like a sister baby," said Emily.
Emily's mum patted her round baby bump.
"We'll just have to wait and see, won't we?"

Well, the baby bump grew. And a little worry started to grow in Emily's mind. And the bigger the baby bump grew, the bigger Emily's worry grew. One day the bump was so huge that Emily couldn't even fit on her mum's lap.

A bit later, Emily came into the kitchen.
"Guess what I've been doing," she said.
"Have you been making a list?" suggested Emily's dad.
"Yes, I have," admitted Emily.
"Is it anything to do with babies?"
"Yes, it is," said Emily.
"Good," said Emily's dad.
"It's not that good," warned Emily.
She settled the guinea pig on her lap and began to read.

A baby is good because...

It is
really tiny.

Its head is soft and snuffly.

You can play pat-a-cake.

When it has grown a bit you
can feed it all kinds of squish.

You can take it out for rides in the buggy.

You can swoosh it through puddles.

You can tickle it to bits!

"Well done!" said Emily's mum.
"Positive thinking," agreed Emily's dad.
"Yes BUT. . ." continued Emily darkly, "you haven't heard the other bit."

cry.

waaah!

It cries if it's hungry.
It cries if it's thirsty.
It cries if it's tired.
It cries if it's hot.
It cries if it wants to do a poo.

"But that's not the worst thing,"
said Emily. "When the baby comes . . .

. . . everyone
will come rushing
round. And it will be
baby this and
baby that and
baby goo goo and
baby blah blah blah.
And I will have to eat left-over squish
and go to school in a babygro and mittens.
Everything will be upside down and
inside out because that's the way
it is when a baby comes
into your house!"

"Oh dear," sighed Emily's mum. "That sounds awful."

"But it's not going to be like that," said Emily's dad. "Come and sit on my lap and I will tell you a story about a baby."
"See!" said Emily triumphantly. "It's already started!
Baby baby blah blah blah!"

"No!" interrupted Emily's dad.
"This story is about **YOU!** May I begin?"
Emily nodded.
"A long time ago there was just Mum and me. We did all kinds of stuff together: walking, dancing, climbing up mountains. We were so happy I couldn't imagine it being any better. But then guess what happened?"

"Me . . . ?" said Emily.
"Yes! But having you didn't stop us
doing things, we just took you along too!"
"Even up mountains?" said Emily suspiciously.
Emily's dad smiled. "Well, maybe not up mountains . . ."
"But we did go on bike rides together," said Emily's mum.
"And now we go skating together," said Emily.
"Exactly! It just gets better and better,
doesn't it?" said Emily's dad.

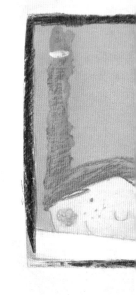

"Maybe," agreed Emily.
"Maybe you could rub a few things off your worry list?"
suggested Emily's mum. "Because you won't really have to
eat squish or go to school in a babygro and mittens."
"That's good," said Emily.

"And . . ." continued Emily's mum,
"we will always make time for cuddles
and laps and stories. Because we will

always love you!

No matter what the BABIES do."

Other Francesca Chessa books for you to enjoy...

Love-a-Duck
written by Alan James Brown
Love-a-Duck has lost his squeak! So when he falls from the bathroom window into the pram, no one notices – not even Jane. But what happens when Love-a-Duck falls from the pram . . . into the POND?!

Holly's Red Boots
Holly can't go out in the snow without her red boots. But where are they? Join her as she searches the house, finding plenty of surprises along the way!

When Brian Was A Lion
written by Carrie Weston
Brian does NOT want to go to Caitlin's party. Worse still, his mum has made him a stuffy, itchy lion suit to wear. But when Brian meets a little alien, suddenly the party takes a surprising turn!